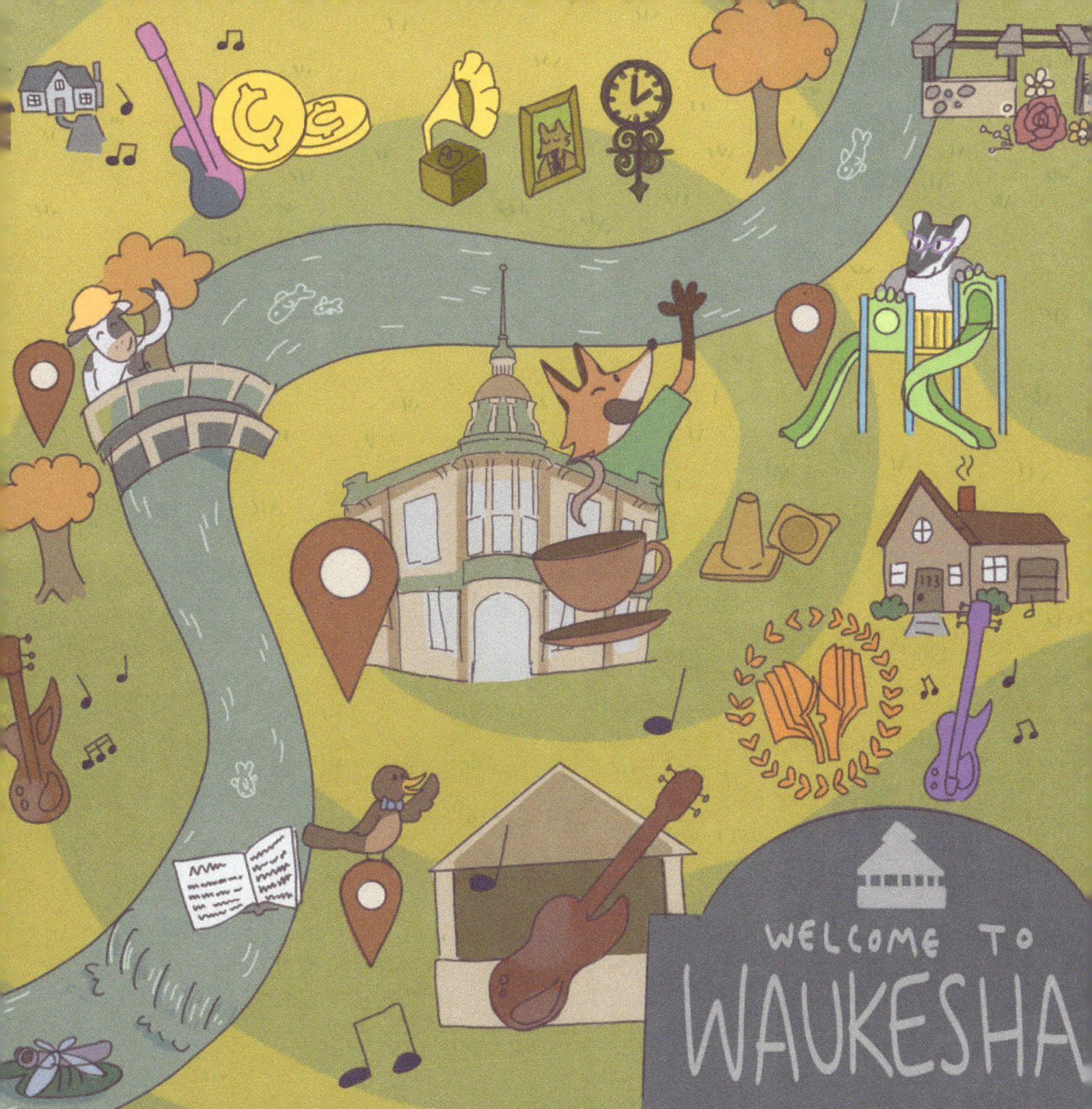

Hi! My name is Java Jo Fox, and today is my birthday! I'm excited to invite my closest friends to celebrate with me. They live in my favorite town, Waukesha.

Can you help me find them?

ONE...
TWO...
THREE!

RODGER!
RODGER!

"There you are, Rodger! What are you up to?"

"Hi, Java Jo! I'm building a new nest. Right now I'm looking for odds and ends to decorate it with," said Rodger.

"That's great! Well, I was wondering...wanna hang out at The Steaming Cup to celebrate my birthday?"

"Oh, Java Jo, I'm sorry! I would, but I really need to finish my nest. Could we another time?"

That was disappointing, but let's head to the Fox River Walk! My friend, Carmine Cow, likes to walk along the trail. Maybe she'll come to the coffee shop with me!
Can you help me find her?
Let's call out her name.

HERE WE GO!

CAN YOU COUNT HOW MANY FLOWERS ARE ON THIS PAGE?

Well, that was a letdown. Can *anybody* hang out with me today? Hopefully, my friend Betty Badger is free to keep me company. She likes to dig at Frame Park. I bet she's there!

Can you help me find her? Ready? Here we go.

"I'm right here. Stop all the yelling!" Betty said.

"Oh, hi, Betty! How's the dig going?"

"It's harder than it looks, but these holes aren't gonna dig themselves!"

"I bet! Hey, I was wondering…do you wanna go to The Cup and hang out for my birthday?"

"No time. These holes have to be dug!" Betty said.

"Okay. Maybe some other time…"

I'm pretty bummed that none of my friends can hang out. I think I'll take the long way back to The Steaming Cup...

I'm still disappointed that my friends can't help celebrate my birthday. Maybe counting the flags on Main Street will boost my spirits?

Today wasn't as fun as I thought it would be. Now that I'm back at The Steaming Cup, I think I'll grab a hot chocolate to go.

HOW MANY UMBRELLAS CAN YOU COUNT?

SURPRISE!

"Oh my goodness! You guys were planning a party all along?"

"We sure were!" said Betty.

"Look at what we made for you!" said Carmine.

"We found flowers and dirt, and now you have a potted plant!" Betty exclaimed.

HAPPY BIRTHDAY!

"And I decorated!" said Rodger. "See all the leaves and twigs? I was collecting them all morning!"

"This is amazing! I thought you were all too busy, but...wow! Thank you so much. Now, let's celebrate together!"

Published by Orange Hat Publishing 2022
ISBN 9781645387251

Copyrighted © 2022 by Agatha Tofte
All Rights Reserved
Help Java Jo Find His Friends in Waukesha
Written by Agatha Tofte
Illustrated by Ariya Monet

This publication and all contents within may not be reproduced or transmitted in any part or in its entirety without the written permission of the author.

www.orangehatpublishing.com

ANSWER KEY!

- 10 LEAVES
- 9 FLOWERS
- 7 HOLES
- 9 CONSTRUCTION CONES
- 7 US FLAGS
- 5 UMBRELLAS

CPSIA information can be obtained
at www.ICGtesting.com
Printed in the USA
BVHW010512041222
653399BV00002B/21